How to Start First Grade

by Cathy Hapka and Ellen Titlebaum

illustrated by Debbie Palen

Random House 🏠 New York

I am Steve.
Today I start
first grade.
That is *real* school.

Dear Parents:

Congratulations! Your child is taking the first steps on an exciting journey. The destination? Independent reading!

STEP INTO READING® will help your child get there. The program offers five steps to reading success. Each step includes fun stories and colorful art or photographs. In addition to original fiction and books with favorite characters, there are Step into Reading Non-Fiction Readers, Phonics Readers and Boxed Sets, Sticker Readers, and Comic Readers—a complete literacy program with something to interest every child.

Learning to Read, Step by Step!

Ready to Read   Preschool–Kindergarten
• big type and easy words • rhyme and rhythm • picture clues
For children who know the alphabet and are eager to begin reading.

Reading with Help   Preschool–Grade 1
• basic vocabulary • short sentences • simple stories
For children who recognize familiar words and sound out new words with help.

Reading on Your Own   Grades 1–3
• engaging characters • easy-to-follow plots • popular topics
For children who are ready to read on their own.

Reading Paragraphs   Grades 2–3
• challenging vocabulary • short paragraphs • exciting stories
For newly independent readers who read simple sentences with confidence.

Ready for Chapters   Grades 2–4
• chapters • longer paragraphs • full-color art
For children who want to take the plunge into chapter books but still like colorful pictures.

STEP INTO READING® is designed to give every child a successful reading experience. The grade levels are only guides; children will progress through the steps at their own speed, developing confidence in their reading. The F&P Text Level on the back cover serves as another tool to help you choose the right book for your child.

Remember, a lifetime love of reading starts with a single step!

*For all the kids who love to try new things
and make new friends
—C.H. & E.T.*

*For Pie, the most popular girl in my school
—D.P.*

Text copyright © 2020 by Catherine A. Hapka and Ellen Titlebaum
Cover art and interior illustrations copyright © 2020 by Debbie Palen

Visit us on the Web!
StepIntoReading.com
rhcbooks.com

Educators and librarians, for a variety of teaching tools, visit us at RHTeachersLibrarians.com

Library of Congress Cataloging-in-Publication Data
Names: Hapka, Cathy, author. | Titlebaum, Ellen, author. | Palen, Debbie,
illustrator.
Title: How to start first grade / by Cathy Hapka and Ellen Titlebaum;
illustrated by Debbie Palen.
Description: First edition. | New York : Random House Children's Books,
[2020] | Series: Step into reading. Step 2, reading with help. |
Audience: Ages 4–6. | Audience: Grades K–1. | Summary: Steve is excited
and happy to be starting "real school" until Hannah, who just moved from
Alaska, captures everyone's attention and his response lands him in the
principal's office.
Identifiers: LCCN 2019030533 (print) | LCCN 2019030534 (ebook) |
ISBN 978-1-5247-1554-0 (trade) | ISBN 978-1-5247-1555-7 (lib. bdg.) |
ISBN 978-1-5247-1556-4 (ebook)
Subjects: CYAC: Schools—Fiction. | Friendship—Fiction.
Classification: LCC PZ7.H1996 Hou 2020 (print) | LCC PZ7.H1996 (ebook) |
DDC [E]—dc23

Printed in the United States of America
10 9 8 7 6 5 4 3 2 1
First Edition

This book has been officially leveled by using the F&P Text Level Gradient™ Leveling System.

I cannot wait!
This will be
the best year yet!

I walk in with
my friend David.
Everyone is happy
to see me.
I love first grade so far.
For sure!

Everyone loves
my stories from summer.
Then Abigail
runs to the window.

"Look!" she cries.

It is a girl

on a dog sled!

Ms. Chen says Hannah
moved here from Alaska.
She asks her to tell us
about herself.

"One time,
my dog and I
raced a bear!"
Hannah says.

Everyone wants to sit
next to Hannah.
"She is cool,"
David says.

"One time, my dog
barked at a
mean bunny," I say.
That is just as cool.

Soon it is time
for show-and-tell.
I go first.

I open my bag.

Oh, no!

My shark fell apart!

I am sad.

It *was* a great shark.

Hannah goes next.
"I always carry
my gold nugget,"
she says.
"I found it myself."

Show-and-Tell

We go outside
for recess.
Everyone wants to see
the gold nugget.
But I do not.
I think it is fake.

Hannah draws
her house in Alaska
with chalk.

It has snow
up to the roof!
"That is fake," I say.
"It is not," she says.

I draw my house.
It can fly
to the moon.
For sure!

David shakes his head.
"That is not
your house,"
he says.

"I am not lying," I cry.

"Hannah is lying!"

Hannah gets mad.

She says she never lies.

She says I am a liar!

We yell at each other

so much that

Ms. Chen sends us

to the principal.

We wait by the office.

Hannah looks scared.

I tell her not to worry.

I have been here
lots of times.

"Thanks," Hannah says.

"Sorry I called you a liar."

"I am sorry, too," I say.
"How did you teach
your dog to pull a sled?"

Hannah tells me
she can teach my dog
to pull one, too.
I tell her about my shark.

Principal Smiley comes out and asks us what is wrong.

"Nothing," Hannah says.

I agree.

I love making new friends.

And I love first grade!